GRANDPA COMES TO STAY

Rob Lewis

First published in the United States of America in 1996
by **MONDO Publishing**

Originally published in the United Kingdom in 1996
by The Bodley Head Children's Books,
an imprint of Random House UK Ltd.

For information contact:
MONDO Publishing
One Plaza Road
Greenvale, New York 11548

Printed in Hong Kong
First Mondo printing, February 1996
96 97 98 99 00 01   9 8 7 6 5 4 3 2 1

Library of Congress Cataloging-in-Publication Data

Lewis, Rob.

Grandpa comes to stay / [written and illustrated by] Rob Lewis.

p.   cm.

"Originally published in the United Kingdom in 1996 by the Bodley Head
Children's Books, and imprint of Random House UK Ltd."—P. 2.

Summary: A young bear and his grandfather share some adventures in
three stories: Peace and quiet for Grandpa, Fish tale, and Grandpa cooks
supper.

ISBN 1-57255-212-3 (pbk. : alk. paper)

[1. Grandfathers—Fiction. 2. Bears—Fiction.] I. Title.

PZ7.L58785Gr   1996

E—dc20   95-50370
                                                              CIP
                                                               AC

PEACE AND QUIET
FOR GRANDPA

"Finley! Don't put your feet on the sofa!" said Mom.

"Pardon?" said Finley.

"TURN THE TELEVISION DOWN!" shouted Mom.

"Now, don't put your feet on the sofa."

"Sorry, Mom," said Finley.

Finley went into the kitchen. He poured himself a glass of milk and cut some cake. Then he watched television again.

"There are cake crumbs everywhere!" said Mom.

"And you have spilled milk on the table!"

"Sorry, Mom," said Finley.

"Now listen carefully," said Mom.
"Grandpa is coming to stay. He has
been ill. He needs peace and quiet.
Noise and mess are not good for him."

"You mean no loud television?" said Finley.

"Exactly," said Mom.

"No feet on the sofa?" said Finley.

"Absolutely not," said Mom.

"No crumbs?" said Finley.

"Not one," said Mom.

"No spilled drinks?" said Finley.

"Not a drop," said Mom.

Grandpa came the next afternoon.

Mom made some tea in the kitchen.

Grandpa turned on the television.

"There's a good game on," he said to Finley.

Grandpa turned the television up VERY LOUD.

"Goal!" he shouted, jumping up and down on the sofa.

"Finley! Turn off that television!" Mom yelled from the kitchen.

"Grandpa doesn't want a lot of noisy football. I hope you don't have your feet on the sofa."

"No, Mom," said Finley.

"Sorry, Finley," said Grandpa.

Mom brought in the tea and cupcakes.

Then she took Grandpa's bags upstairs.

Grandpa was a bit bored.

"Watch this, Finley," he said. "I can balance
my cupcake on the edge of my cup."

Flop! The cupcake fell into Grandpa's tea.

"Whoops," he said.

Mom came downstairs.

"Finley, I told you not to spill any drinks
or drop crumbs!

Grandpa doesn't want a lot of mess
around when he's been ill," she said.

Mom went to get a cloth.

"I only had a cold," said Grandpa.

"Sorry, Finley."

In the evening Mom and Dad went to a party.

"Are you sure you're well enough to baby-sit?" said Mom.

"Yes," said Grandpa.

Grandpa looked at Finley.

"Tonight," he said, "we will put our feet on the sofa.

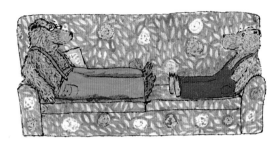

We will turn the television up loud.

We will drop crumbs everywhere and
we will spill drinks on the table."

And they did.

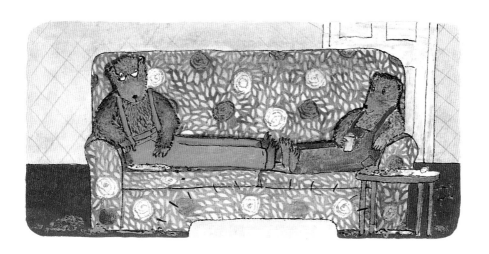

But they cleaned up the mess before
Mom and Dad got home.

FISH TALE

Finley and Grandpa went fishing.

They climbed the hill.

"Hurry up, Grandpa," called Finley.

Finley ran down the other side of the hill.

They crossed the river on stepping stones.

"Careful, Grandpa," said Finley. "You might fall in."

They sat down on the river bank under a shady tree.

"Shall I put the bait on the hook?" asked Finley.

"If you like," said Grandpa.

"Being old can't be much fun," said Finley.

"Why ever do you think that?" asked Grandpa.

"You get slow and shaky don't you?" said Finley. "It must be hard to catch fish."

"In that case," said Grandpa, "how about a competition? *You* fish here and I will fish up the river a little way. We will see who has the most fish by lunchtime."

Grandpa took his fishing bag and his rod and wandered along the riverbank until he was just out of sight. Finley started to fish. There weren't many fish in the river. By lunchtime, all he had caught was a couple of little fish.

Finley went to find Grandpa. He followed
the path along the riverbank but there
was no sign of Grandpa anywhere.
"Maybe Grandpa got lost," Finley said
to himself.

Then he saw Grandpa's hat and rod lying on the path.

"Oh no!" Finley wailed. "Grandpa has fallen into the river."

Finley wondered what to do. "Why didn't
I look after him properly," he cried.
Just then Grandpa strolled up along
the path.

"Where have you been?" said Finley crossly.

"I found a good place to get fish," smiled Grandpa.

Grandpa showed Finley his bag. The bag was full of fish. They were not little like Finley's fish. They were big and shiny. Finley was amazed.

"How did you catch those?" he said.

"It takes many years of skill," said Grandpa. "You need to learn where to fish and how to fish properly."

"You are clever, Grandpa," said Finley.

"Will you teach me how to fish properly?"

"Maybe," said Grandpa.

Grandpa noticed the fish store bag

sticking out of his pocket.

He quickly stuffed it back in again.

"Let's build a fire and cook these fish for dinner," he said.

GRANDPA COOKS SUPPER

Mom came home from work.

"I'm too tired to cook," she said.

"Let's get take-out," said Dad.

"It's OK," said Grandpa. "I will cook."

"Are you sure?" said Mom.

"Of course he's sure," said Finley.

"In that case, thank you," said Mom.

"There are eggs in the refrigerator
for an omelet. Finley can help."
Finley and Grandpa went into the
kitchen.

"What flavor omelet are we going to make?" asked Finley.

"Just fetch me the frying pan," said Grandpa.

Grandpa put the frying pan on the stove. He heated some oil in the pan.

"Eight eggs please," he said, "and some milk."

Finley fetched the eggs and milk from
the refrigerator.

Grandpa put the eggs and milk in the pan.

"But Grandpa!" said Finley. "You don't
put the egg shells in as well!"

"I do," said Grandpa.

"It's going to be a crunchy mushroom and
cheese omelet."

Grandpa added the mushrooms and cheese. He tasted the omelet.

"Hmm… It's not spicy enough," he said. "Fetch the mustard, Finley."

Grandpa emptied the jar of mustard onto the omelet. He tasted it again.

"Hmmm… It's not sweet enough," he said.
"Fetch the jelly."

Grandpa emptied the jar of jelly onto
the omelet.

"Hmmm… Not enough filling," said
Grandpa. "Fetch me a bag of fries from
the freezer."

Grandpa emptied the fries onto the omelet.

"Aren't you going to cook them first?" asked Finley.

"Remember, it's a crunchy omelet," said Grandpa. "Fries are crunchier frozen."

Grandpa tasted the omelet again.

"Hmmm... Not sharp enough," he said.

"Bring me some lemons."

Grandpa sliced the lemons onto the
omelet.

"Hmmm... Not chewy enough," he said.

"Bring me the bag of raisins."

Grandpa emptied the bag of raisins
onto the omelet.

"Hmmm… Not creamy enough," said Grandpa. "Find me two cups of pudding." He emptied the cups onto the omelet.

"Hmmm… Not colorful enough," said Grandpa. "Find me the tomato ketchup and grape juice."

Grandpa emptied the ketchup and juice onto the omelet.

"But Grandpa!" said Finley. "There's no more room in the pan!"

"That means the omelet is ready," said Grandpa.

Grandpa put the omelet onto plates.

"Only a little bit for me," said Finley.

Everyone tasted the omelet.

"Quite spicy," said Dad.

"Quite chewy," said Mom.

"Quite sharp," said Finley.

"Lovely and sweet and colorful and
crunchy and creamy!" said Grandpa.

"We're not hungry," said Dad and Finley.

"I'm too tired to eat," said Mom.

"In that case, I'll have it all," said Grandpa.

He emptied their plates onto his plate.

Mom and Dad gave Finley a look.

"Tomorrow we'll have take-out,"
they said.